SOLOMON AND FRIENDS™
LEARN ABOUT
CHRISTMAS

BOOK 5

Kids Learn About Luke 2:11

"...a Savior has been born to you; He is Christ the Lord."

This book belongs to:

_____

NOTE: Wonder Paws are points where you can pause and reflect with your child on what's happening in the story, and relate it to something real in your child's life. Use these engagement points to see things from your child's point of view and get them wondering about God.

One *cold, wintry* night, Solomon and his family decorated their Christmas tree.

Solomon said, "I can't wait until Christmas. I can't wait to get *ALL* those presents."

Mr. Nehemiah said, "Actually, Solomon, there's a verse in the Bible that tells us what Christmas is really all about. Luke 2:11 says, 'Today in the town of David a Savior has been born to you; He is Christ the Lord.' That's *the real meaning of Christmas.*"

When they finished decorating the tree, Mr. Nehemiah opened his Bible and read *the story of Christmas — Jesus' birthday —* and how God sent Jesus, His only Son, into the world because He loved us *so much*.

Solomon asked, "If Christmas is Jesus' birthday, why do we give presents?"

Mr. Nehemiah said, "Solomon, God gave us His gift of Jesus because **He loves us and wants *everyone* to know Him.** At Christmas, we celebrate and follow God's loving example by giving gifts to those we love."

Why is Christmas so special?

Wonder PAWS

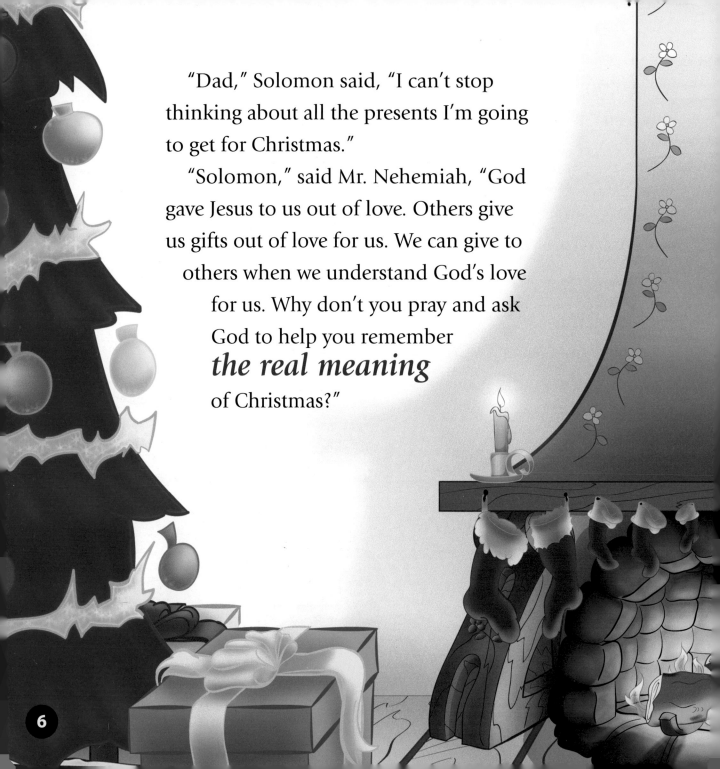

"Dad," Solomon said, "I can't stop thinking about all the presents I'm going to get for Christmas."

"Solomon," said Mr. Nehemiah, "God gave Jesus to us out of love. Others give us gifts out of love for us. We can give to others when we understand God's love for us. Why don't you pray and ask God to help you remember *the real meaning* of Christmas?"

Solomon bowed his head. *"God, You sent such **a great gift** when You sent **Jesus**. Please help me to remember how much **You love me**, and **help me love others**. Help me to **give gifts to** them out of love. Amen."*

Why do we give gifts at Christmas?

Wonder PAWS

On Sunday, Solomon ran to his Sunday School class. He *s l i d   i n t o* a seat next to Reuben. "We set up our Christmas tree," he said. "You know what that means — time to make out

THE CHRISTMAS LIST."

Benjamin nodded. "Yeah, yeah, yeah! I made up my list last night." He began H O P P I N G through the chairs. "You should see it. It's *three* pages long!"

Reuben started laughing. "I want *MORE* treasures and gifts." His eyes got big. *"Gifts that sparkle."*

Solomon shook his head. "I'm still working on my list."

Eli popped out of Solomon's pocket. **"Solomon,** remember that *Christmas isn't just about gifts.* **It's about Jesus** being born!" he said. God gave His Son Jesus because He loves us and wants everyone to know Him."

How much does God love you?

wonder PAWS

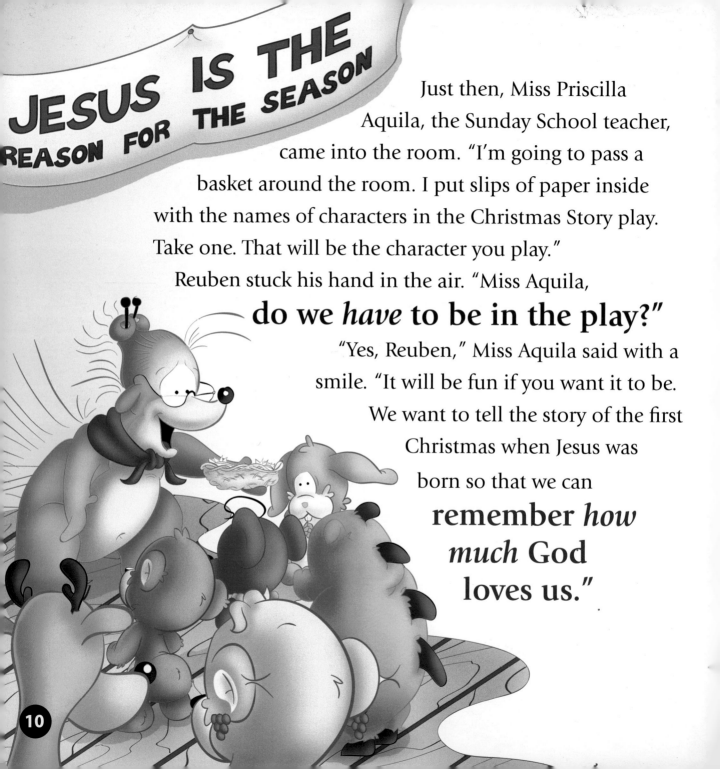

JESUS IS THE REASON FOR THE SEASON

Just then, Miss Priscilla Aquila, the Sunday School teacher, came into the room. "I'm going to pass a basket around the room. I put slips of paper inside with the names of characters in the Christmas Story play. Take one. That will be the character you play."

Reuben stuck his hand in the air. "Miss Aquila, **do we *have* to be in the play?**"

"Yes, Reuben," Miss Aquila said with a smile. "It will be fun if you want it to be. We want to tell the story of the first Christmas when Jesus was born so that we can **remember *how much* God loves us.**"

When the basket came to him, Solomon took a piece of paper. Then he quickly peeked at the paper. **JOSEPH.** Solomon frowned. That meant he'd have to learn *a lot* of lines.

Benjamin leaned over. **"I'M** playing one of the wise men."

"So am I!" exclaimed Reuben. **"We get to bring** PRESENTS *and* TREASURES **to** *baby Jesus."*

"Who did you get, Solomon?" asked Benjamin. ***"Huh? Huh? Huh?"***

"I'm playing Joseph," Solomon said.

On the way home from church, Mr. Nehemiah asked Solomon and Sara who they were going to play in the **Christmas Story play**.

"I'm a shepherd,"
said Sara excitedly.
"I'm playing Joseph," said Solomon.
"There are a lot of lines to learn."

The night of the **Christmas play,** everyone scurried around. Solomon peeked into the church auditorium. The church was **FULL.** He saw his mom and dad in the front row. The front of the church was decorated like the town of Bethlehem, where Jesus was born.

Miss Aquila called everyone into one of the classrooms. "Class, let's pray before we start the play."

14

"Dear God," Miss Aquila prayed, "please help us remember our lines. And please,

God, let this play remind us of *what Christmas is really ALL about — Your special gift of Jesus* and Your love for us.

Thank You for being a loving and caring God.

Amen."

Luke came out on stage. The lights
went out, and a spotlight shone on him.

"'Today in the town of David *a Savior* has been
born to you; *He is Christ the LORD*,' Luke 2:11."

When he finished, he smiled a
t o o t h y smile at the crowd
and bowed. Everyone giggled.

Rebecca, who was playing Mary, Jesus' mother, was on the back of David, the donkey.

Solomon took a deep breath and knocked on the door of the inn.

Luke opened the door. He bellowed,

"THERE'S NO ROOM IN THE INN FOR YOU!"

"But — but — but my wife is tired, and she's going to have a baby. Please let us stay," Solomon stammered.

"OK." Luke pointed. "You can stay in my barn, **but it** *doesn't* **smell very good.**"

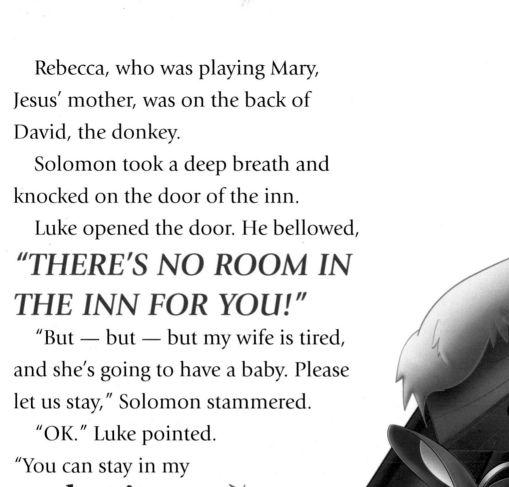

Luke led Solomon and Rebecca to
the corner of the stage. There was a basket
filled with straw. Rebecca stood on one
side of the basket and Solomon stood
on the other side. Baby Ezekiel, who
was playing **the baby Jesus,**
lay inside the basket.

At the other side of
the stage, Opossum Paul
hung from the rafters above
the stage. A light shone on him.

"**Today in the town of
David *a Savior* has been born
to you; He is *Christ the Lord*,**" he said.
"**God sent Him as *a truly special gift
to us* so that EVERYONE could come
to know Him.**"

Then all the shepherds came in to see *the baby Jesus.* Sara led the small lambs from the pres... Sunday School class onto the stage. The last little lamb excitedly ran up the step. He t r i p p e d and fell **FLAT** on his face. He got up and giggled. Then he followed the other lambs onto the stage.

The audience giggled, too.

Once all the shepherds got on stage, they **WORSHIPPED** *the baby Jesus.*

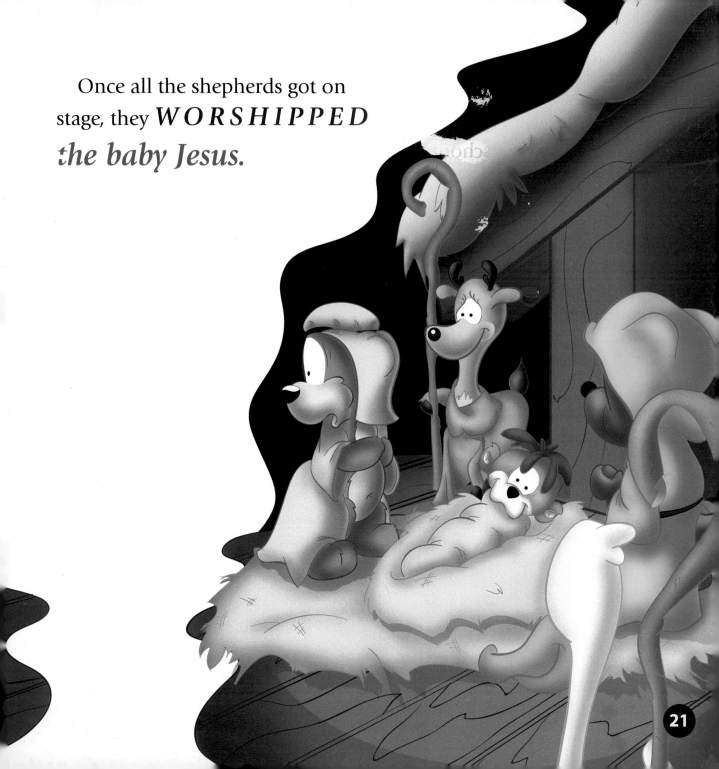

ACT 2: The Wise Men

Luke marched up to Solomon and Rebecca. *"THERE ARE SOME WISE GUYS HERE TO SEE YOU,"* he announced, *"AND THEY WANT TO WORSHIP YOUR BABY JESUS."*

Again, giggles rippled through the audience.

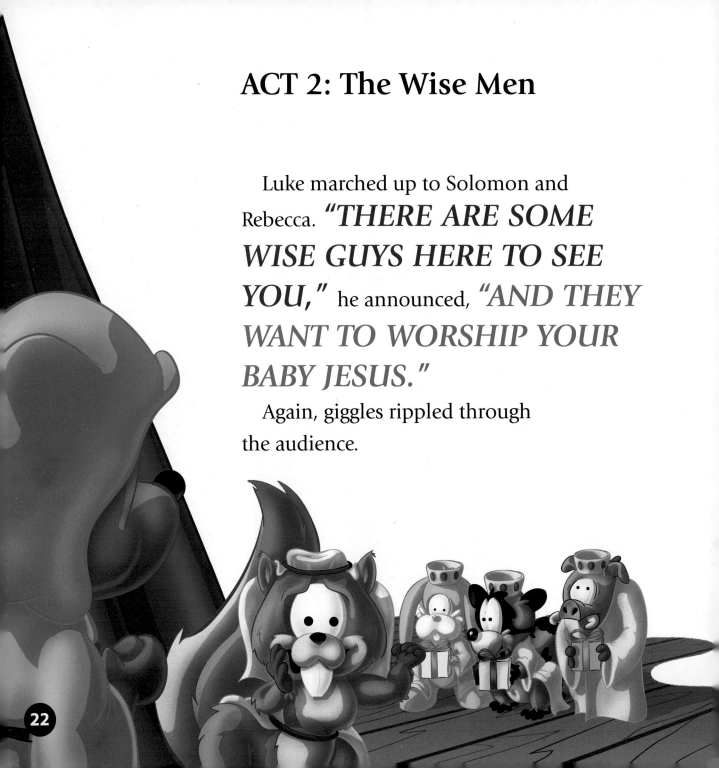

Reuben, playing one of the wise men, stepped out from backstage. Reuben brought a gift over to *the baby Jesus.* With a serious look on his face, he knelt down and presented the gift.

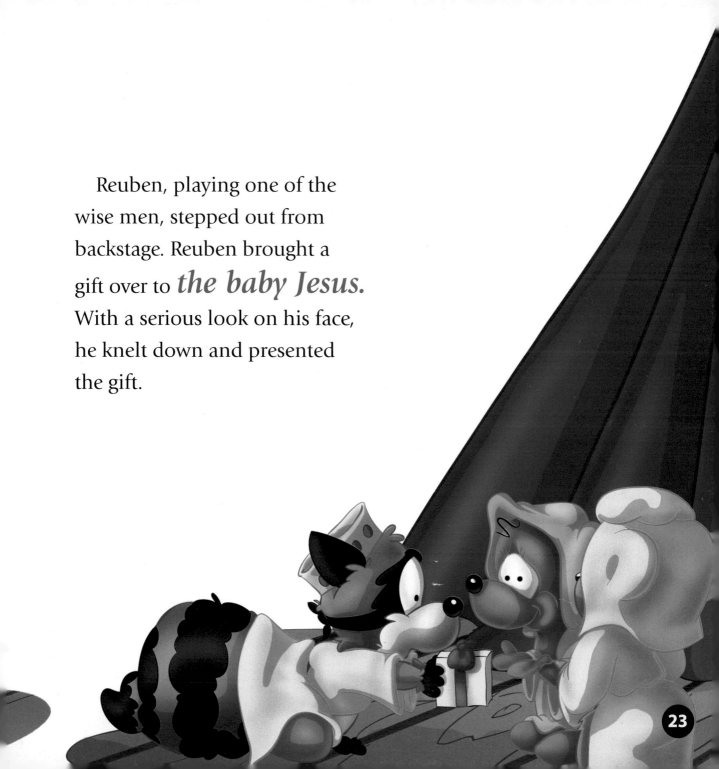

"Here's a gift for the baby Jesus." Reuben looked at Miss Aquila. She whispered something, and he turned back to the manger. "Oh yeah. God gave us Jesus because He loves us so much and wants everyone to know Him." He turned back to Miss Aquila. "Did I say it right?"

She nodded.

Rebecca smiled as she played Jesus' mother, Mary.

"I thank you for this gift."

Solomon, playing Joseph, thanked him also.

Why did God send Jesus?

wonder PAWS

Reuben faced the audience.
He looked at Miss Aquila and cleared
his throat. "We all like receiving gifts
on Christmas. *But* **Christmas is
special** *because* **God sent
Jesus.** God gave Jesus because He
loves us *so much.*"

The audience stood to its feet and *C-L-A-P-P-E-D.*

Solomon saw his dad smiling a **BIG SMILE** and his mom wiping a *t e a r from her eye.*

After the play ended, Rebecca ran up to Solomon. "Solomon, I have a Christmas present for you! **I give this to you *with love*,** just like God gave Jesus to us so that everyone could know Him."

Solomon *blushed* and said, "Wow! Thank you, Rebecca. That was a *very* kind and loving thing to do."

After she left, Eli said, "Solomon, you accepted that gift from Rebecca just like we should **accept God's gift of Jesus** — with an open heart."

Who are the people you love?

Wonder PAWS

On Christmas morning, Solomon woke up early and saw the rising sun **SHINING BRIGHTLY** on the snow. He said to Eli, "I can't wait until my family sees the gifts I chose for them.

I want them to know *how much* I love them,

just like God showed He loved me when He sent Jesus." He grabbed his Bible and ran to his parents' room. "Mom? Dad?"

"Come in, Solomon," his dad said s l *e e e e e* p i l y.

"Merry Christmas!"

said Solomon. "Can we read the Christmas Story *before* we open our presents?"

Mr. Nehemiah smiled. "That's a great idea, Solomon."

The family gathered downstairs around the Christmas tree. Mr. Nehemiah opened his Bible and began to read the Christmas story from Luke 2:1-20. When he got to verse 11, Solomon and Sara joined in:

"Today in the town of David A SAVIOR has been born to you; He is Christ the Lord."

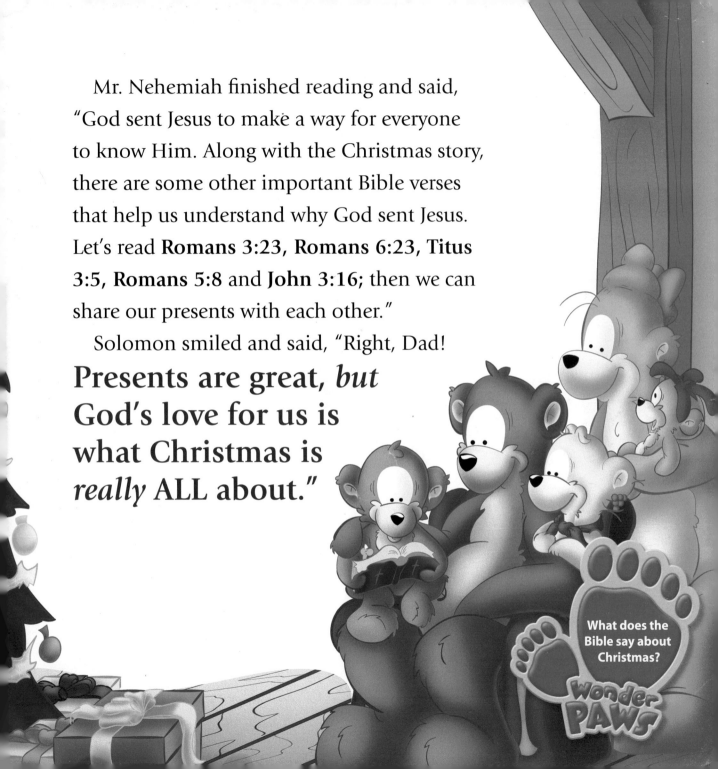

Mr. Nehemiah finished reading and said, "God sent Jesus to make a way for everyone to know Him. Along with the Christmas story, there are some other important Bible verses that help us understand why God sent Jesus. Let's read **Romans 3:23, Romans 6:23, Titus 3:5, Romans 5:8** and **John 3:16;** then we can share our presents with each other."

Solomon smiled and said, "Right, Dad! **Presents are great, *but* God's love for us is what Christmas is *really* ALL about."**

What does the Bible say about Christmas?

Wonder PAWS

SALUDOS NAVIDEÑOS